Fairytale Twists

Jack
and the
Bean Pie

Written by Laura North
Illustrated by Mike Phillips

Crabtree Publishing Company
www.crabtreebooks.com

Crabtree Publishing Company
www.crabtreebooks.com
1-800-387-7650

PMB 59051, 350 Fifth Ave.
59th Floor,
New York, NY 10118

616 Welland Ave.
St. Catharines, ON
L2M 5V6

Published by Crabtree Publishing in 2014

Series editor: Melanie Palmer
Editor: Crystal Sikkens
Notes to adults: Reagan Miller
Series advisor: Catherine Glavina
Series designer: Peter Scoulding
**Production coordinator and
    Prepress technician:** Margaret Amy Salter
Print coordinator: Margaret Amy Salter

Text © Laura North 2010
Illustrations © Mike Phillips 2010

The rights of Laura North to be
identified as the author and
Mike Phillips as the illustrator of
this Work have been asserted.

First published in 2010
by Franklin Watts
(A division of Hachette
Children's Books)

Printed in the
U.S.A./092014/CG20140808

**Library and Archives Canada
Cataloguing in Publication**

North, Laura, author
    Jack and the bean pie / written by Laura
North ; illustrated by Mike Phillips.

(Tadpoles: fairytale twists)
Issued in print and electronic formats.
ISBN 978-0-7787-0441-6 (bound).--ISBN 978-0-7787-
0449-2 (pbk.).--ISBN 978-1-4271-7561-8 (pdf).--ISBN
978-1-4271-7553-3 (html)

I. Phillips, Mike, 1961-, illustrator II. Title.

PZ7.N815Ja 2014   C813'.6   C2013-908327-8
                                                    C2013-908328-6

**Library of Congress
Cataloging-in-Publication Data**

CIP available at Library of Congress

This story is based on the traditional fairy tale,
Jack and the Beanstalk, but with a new twist.
Can you make up your own twist for the story?

Once upon a time, a boy
named Jack lived in a tiny
house with his mother.

They had no money and just
ate vegetables from their garden.
But Jack was very good at cooking.
He made delicious bean pies.

One day, he took
the pies to the
market to sell.

6

"I'll buy your pies," said an old man. "But I can only pay with these magic beans." Jack agreed and raced home with them.

Jack's mother was furious.
"We need gold coins, not these
useless beans!" she shouted.

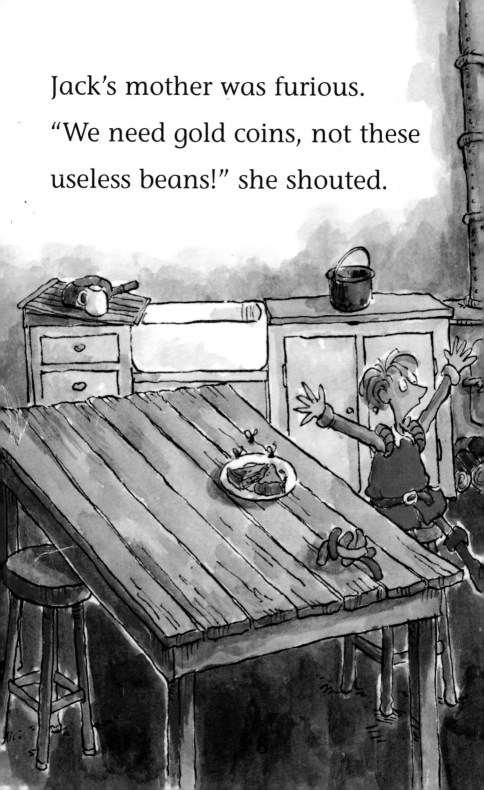

She grabbed some beans and
threw them out of the window
in anger.

The next day, there was a huge
beanstalk in the garden. The
beans were magic after all!

"I wonder what's at the top?"
thought Jack. He started to climb,
up and up, into the clouds, until...

…he found another world! There were enormous flowers, the size of trees. He saw a bee the size of a horse!

Then a voice boomed,

"Fe fi fo fum..!"

"What's that?" thought Jack.

The voice got louder.

"Fe fi fo fum!
I smell the blood
of an Englishman!"

Suddenly, a huge hairy giant stood in front of Jack.

He picked up Jack in one hand.

"Got you!" the giant growled.

Jack was terrified!

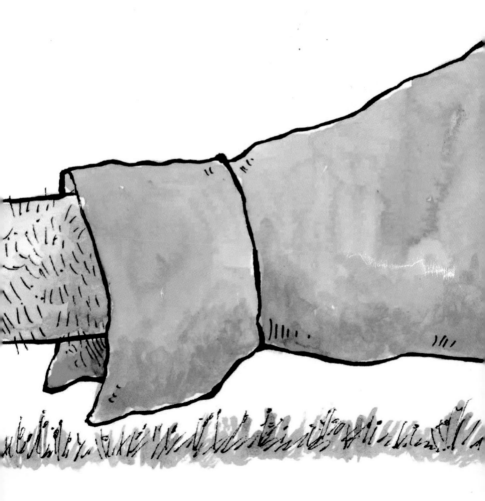

Jack had a few magic beans left in his pocket. He threw them at the giant and hoped they were still magic.

"Yum!" said the giant. "I love beans! They taste much better than humans."

Then the giant started to cry.
"I don't want to eat you at all,"
he sobbed. Big tears fell on Jack.
"The other giants make me
eat people. What can I do?"

21

Jack felt sorry for the giant.

"I've got an idea," he said.

"I can cook great pies. Let's tell the other giants they are human pies, but really fill them with beans!"

"Come and get your human pies!" shouted Jack.

The hungry giants soon arrived.

As the giants gobbled up the pies, Jack bravely jumped up. "SURPRISE! The pies are full of beans, not people!" he said.

"But this is the best pie I've ever had!" roared one giant.

"More bean pies!" they shouted.

The pies were so tasty that the giants forgot about eating people.

Soon Jack became rich and famous from his bean pies. The giants never tried to eat humans again.

Puzzle 1

Put these pictures in the correct order. Which event is the most important? Try writing the story in your own words. Use your imagination to put your own "twist" on the story!

Puzzle 2

1. I'd like to buy your pies.

2. I have a very strong sense of smell.

3. I love cooking!

4. I wonder if the beans are magic?

5. I don't have any coins.

6. I don't like the taste of humans.

Match the speech bubbles to the correct character in the story. Turn the page to check your answers.

Notes for adults

TADPOLES: Fairytale Twists are engaging, imaginative stories designed for early fluent readers. The books may also be used for read-alouds or shared reading with young children.

TADPOLES: Fairytale Twists are humorous stories with a unique twist on traditional fairy tales. Each story can be compared to the original fairy tale, or appreciated on its own. Fairy tales are a key type of literary text found in the Common Core State Standards.

THE FOLLOWING PROMPTS BEFORE, DURING, AND AFTER READING SUPPORT LITERACY SKILL DEVELOPMENT AND CAN ENRICH SHARED READING EXPERIENCES:

1. **Before Reading**: Do a picture walk through the book, previewing the illustrations. Ask the reader to predict what will happen in the story. For example, ask the reader what he or she thinks the twist in the story will be.

2. **During Reading**: Encourage the reader to use context clues and illustrations to determine the meaning of unknown words or phrases.

3. **During Reading**: Have the reader stop midway through the book to revisit his or her predictions. Does the reader wish to change his or her predictions based on what they have read so far?

4. **During and After Reading**: Encourage the reader to make different connections:
   Text-to-Text: How is this story similar to/different from other stories you have read?
   Text-to-World: How are events in this story similar to/different from things that happen in the real world?
   Text-to-Self: Does a character or event in this story remind you of anything in your own life?

5. **After Reading**: Encourage the child to reread the story and to retell it using his or her own words. Invite the child to use the illustrations as a guide.

VISIT WWW.CRABTREEBOOKS.COM FOR OTHER CRABTREE BOOKS.

Answers
Puzzle 1

The correct order is: 1e, 2f, 3a, 4b, 5d, 6c

Puzzle 2

Jack: 3, 4
The giant: 2, 6
The old man: 1, 5